HAPPY HONEY

HAPPY CHRISTMAS, HONEY!

HAPPY CHRISTMAS, HONEY!

written by Laura Godwin

pictures by Jane Chapman

Aladdin Paperbacks

New York   London   Toronto   Sydney   Singapore

*For the children at the Caroline
School in Alberta, Canada
—L. G.*

*For Olivia and Georgie
—J. C.*

First Aladdin Paperbacks edition October 2002
Text copyright © 2002 by Laura Godwin
Illustrations copyright © 2002 by Jane Chapman

ALADDIN PAPERBACKS
An imprint of Simon & Schuster Children's Publishing Division
1230 Avenue of the Americas
New York, NY 10020

Also available in a Margaret K. McElderry hardcover edition.
The Library of Congress has cataloged the hardcover edition as follows:
Library of Congress Cataloging-in-Publication Data
Godwin, Laura.
Happy Christmas, Honey! / written by Laura Godwin ; pictures by Jane Chapman.
p. cm. — (Happy Honey ; 4)
Summary: Honey the cat and Happy the dog celebrate Christmas in their own way.
ISBN 0-689-84714-9 (hc.)
[1. Christmas—Fiction. 2. Cats—Fiction. 3. Dogs—Fiction.]
I. Chapman, Jane, ill. II. Title.
PZ7.G5438 Har 2002
[E]—dc21
2001044119

ISBN 0-689-84764-5 (Aladdin pbk.)

Christmas will come soon.

Honey wants to help.

Honey wants to help
put up the Christmas tree.

Oh, no!

No, no, Honey!

Honey wants to help
make Christmas cookies.

Oh, no!

No, no, Honey!

Honey wants to help
with the Christmas presents.

Oh, no!

No, no, Honey!

Honey wants to help
sing Christmas songs.

Fa la la la la.
Meow, meow, meow.

Oh, no!

No, no, Honey!

Come here, Honey.

Come here

and help Happy.

Happy does not want to help
put up the Christmas tree.

He does not want to help
make Christmas cookies.

He does not want to help
with the Christmas presents.

He does not want to help
sing Christmas songs.

Happy wants
to wait for Santa.

Will Honey help?

Honey will help Happy
wait for Santa.

But will Santa come?

Meow, meow.

Yes, Honey, yes!

Santa did come.

Woof, woof.

Happy Christmas, Honey!